CONTENTS

6	Welcome to the Fam!	42	What's your Soul Colour?
8	BFF Super Search	44	The Best Year Eva!
10	Meet Cotton Candy Sweetie	46	Colour Creations
12	All the Colours	48	Meet Sunset Orange Surfer
13	Trace It!	50	Colour Queen!
14	How Odd!	52	Super Shadows
16	Meet Crayellow Cutie	53	Say Cheese!
18	Colour by Numbers	54	Colour my Feelings!
20	Family Portraits!	56	Fabulous Fashion!
22	Meet Electric Lime Skater	58	10 Ways to be Creative Every Day!
24	Count in Colour!	60	Loud and Proud
25	Meet you Later!	61	Pieces of Puzzles
26	This is My Troop!	62	The Finishing Touches!
28	Meet Precious Periwinkle	64	Meet Sky Blue Dreamer
30	Perfect Patterns	66	Colour Therapy
31	No Bars!	68	Shh! Top Secret!
32	Doodle a Daydream	70	Meet Wild Stawberry Star
34	Meet Orchid Blossom	72	Fabulous Gift Bag
36	Look Closer!	74	Art Forever
38	Artsy Vibes	75	Words for Life
39	Which B.B. Are You Twinning With?	76	Answers
40	Meet Jazzberry Jamm Jewel		

L.O.L. SURPRISE! LOVES Crayola
ANNUAL 2025

Published 2024. Little Brother Books Ltd, Ground Floor, 23 Southernhay East, Exeter, Devon EX1 1QL
books@littlebrotherbooks.co.uk | www.littlebrotherbooks.co.uk
Printed in China.
Little Brother Books, 77 Camden Street Lower, Dublin, D02 XE80
The Little Brother Books trademark, email and website addresses, are the sole and exclusive properties of Little Brother Books Limited.

© MGA Entertainment, Inc.
L.O.L. SURPRISE!™ is a trademark of MGA in the U.S. and other countries. All logos, names, characters, likenesses, images, slogans, and packaging appearance are the property of MGA. Used under license by Little Brother Books Ltd.

©2024 CRAYOLA, EASTON, PA 18044-0431.
Crayola™, Serpentine Design™ and Chevron Design™ are trademarks of Crayola used under license.

HOW ODD!

1 Which Crayola Cutie doesn't have a match?

The L.O.L. that doesn't have a match is... ....

2 Which picture of Sunset Orange Surfer is different to the others?

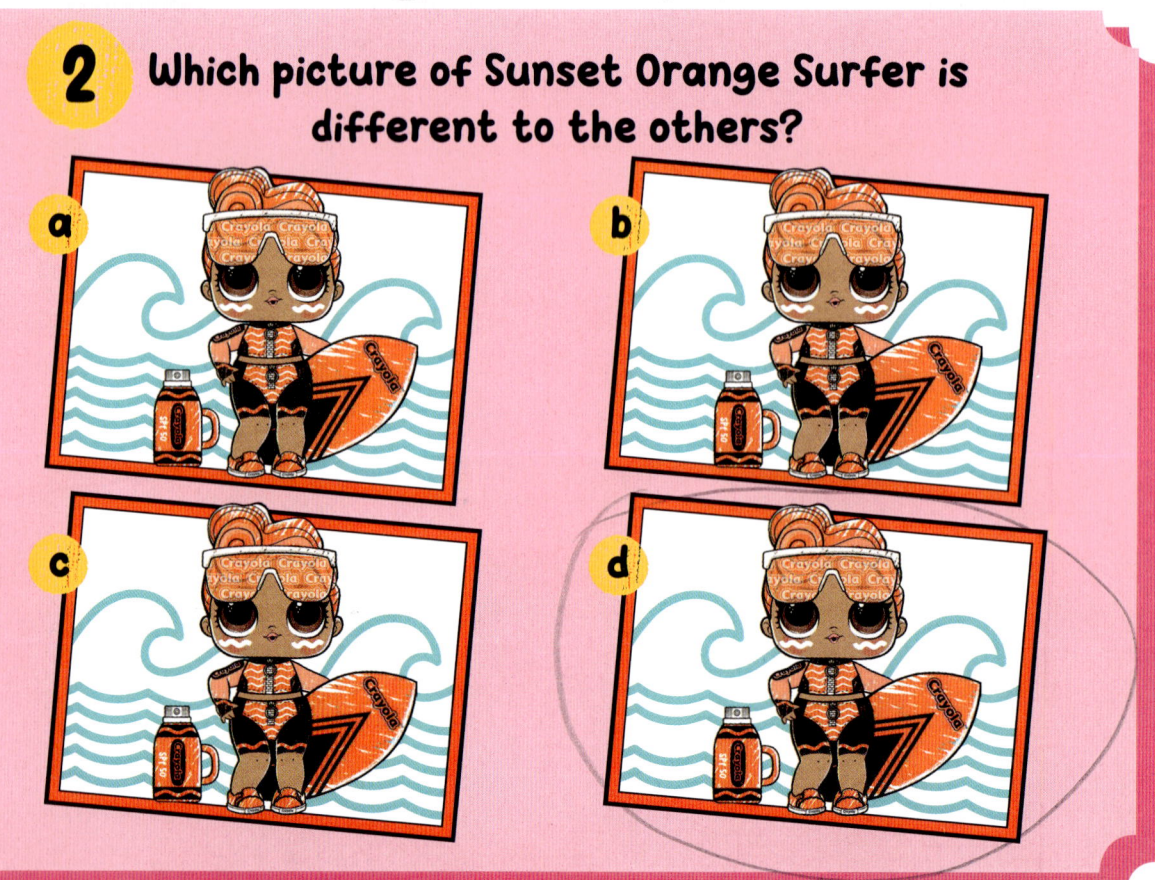

Answers on pages 76–77. ©MGA ©2024 Crayola

Something's not quite right at the Crayola HQ!

GRAB A CRAYOLA SUPER TIP PEN AND GET SPOTTING! CIRCLE THE CORRECT ANSWER FOR EACH PUZZLE.

3. Which of Electric Lime Skater's hats is the odd one out?

a
b
c
d

4. Which two pictures are the same?

a
b
c
d

©MGA ©2024 Crayola

COLOUR BY NUMBERS

FAMILY PORTRAITS!

See if you can doodle your own photo wall!

Grab a pencil and see if you can sketch the L.O.L.s into the frames.

WE'RE ALL

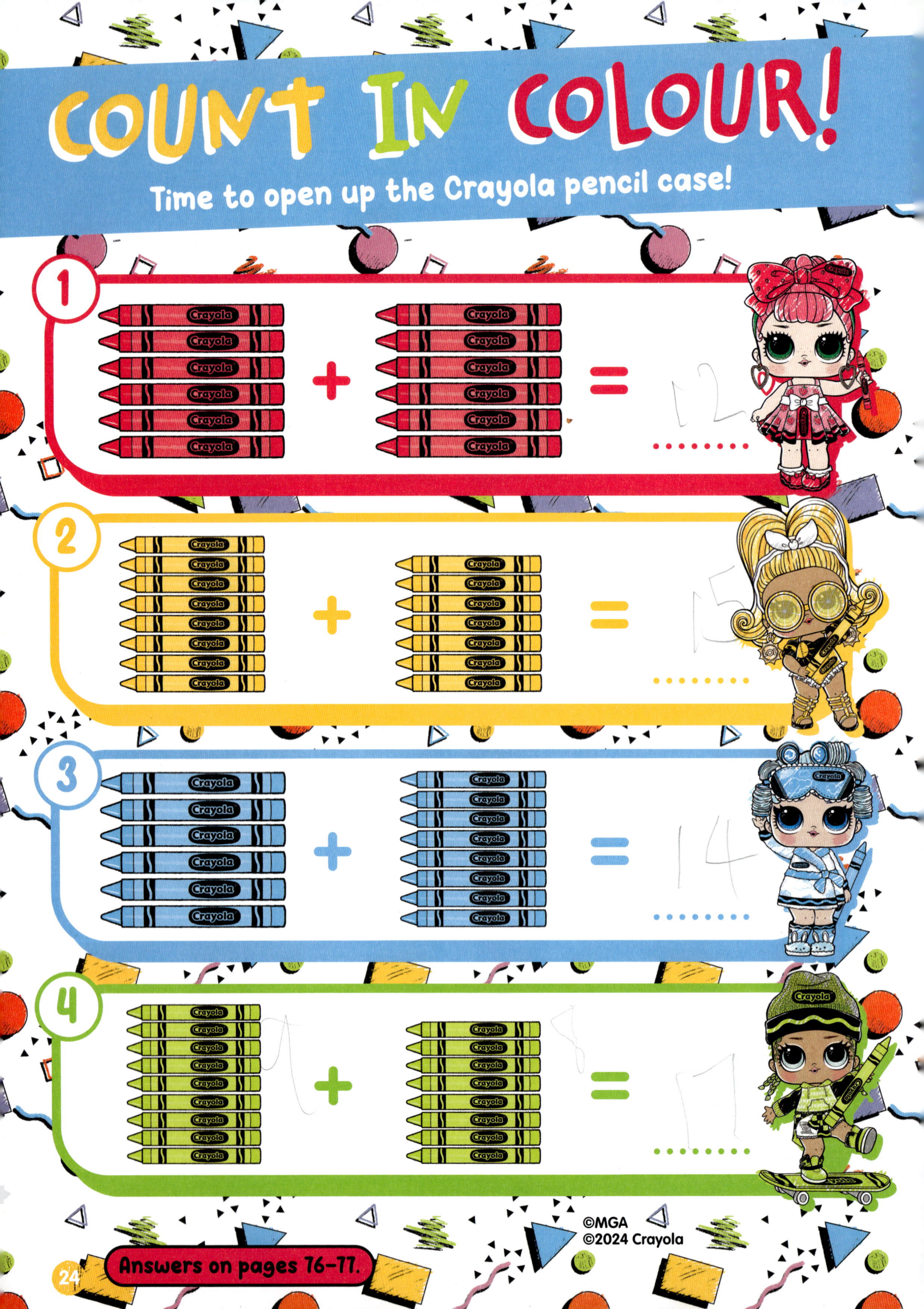

THIS IS MY TROOP!

B.B.s that play together, stay together!

DROPPING BEATS!

Which two beat boxes are the same? Draw a circle around the two pictures that match.

©MGA ©2024 Crayola

NO BARS! 📶 WHO'S CALLING THE B.B.S?

Unscramble the pictures then draw lines to match each phone to the correct L.O.L.

1

2

3

4

5

a. Orchid Blossom

b. Jazzberry Jamm Jewel

c. Electric Lime Skater

d. Crayellow Cutie

e. Precious Periwinkle

Answers on pages 76-77.

DOODLE A DAYDREAM

Dream the day away!

Wow, this one will be amazing!

SO COOL!

Let your imagination run free!

©MGA
©2024 Crayola

LOOK CLOSER!

Draw lines to match all the close ups to their place in the pictures.

EAGLE EYES AT THE READY!

2

1 2 3 4

Answers on pages 76–77.

©MGA ©2024 Crayola

WHICH B.B. ARE YOU TWINNING WITH?

ARE YOU MORE TOUCHDOWN OR SUPA STAR?

TICK 3 STATEMENTS THAT YOU AGREE WITH.

- ✓ Sporty style is my favourite.
- ✓ I like to keep things simple.
- ✓ I'm the best BFF a B.B. could wish for!
- ✓ I love accessories, bows and bangles – the more the merrier!
- ✓ I like sparkly, shiny and colourful vibes!
- ✓ I love to look after all my gal B.B.s!

SQUAD GOALS

SHINE BRIGHT

IF YOU TICKED MOSTLY RED STATEMENTS...

...You're twinning with Touchdown! You're a gal that likes to keep things low key and practical – because you're always on the move!

IF YOU TICKED MOSTLY BLUE STATEMENTS...

...You're twinning with Supa Star! You two would be the life and soul of any L.O.L. party. You both love to get dressed up, and you want to make sure that all the other B.B.s have the best time!

MEET JAZZBERRY JAMM JEWEL

THIS B.B. IS A REAL GEM!

WHICH PANEL CONTAINS THE LETTERS TO SPELL JAZZBERRY? TICK THE CORRECT ONE.

a)
J Z Y
Z B A R
R   A

b)
A R R
Z B E Y
Z   J

c)
Z I R
B Z E J
A   R

Answers on pages 76–77.

©MGA
©2024 Crayola

GRAB YOUR CRAYOLA TOOLS AND COLOUR HER IN.

JAZZBERRY JAMM JEWEL KNOWS THAT A BOW IS ALWAYS A GOOD LOOK.

HER FIERCE SHADES OF PINK ARE NEVER OUT OF FASHION.

©2024 Crayola ©MGA

WHAT'S YOUR SOUL COLOUR?

Circle the option that best describes you to find out!

YOUR HAIR
- a. Bold and trendy
- b. Tied back
- c. Long and shiny
- d. Short and spiky

YOUR DREAM JOB
- a. Film star
- b. Athelete
- c. Fashion designer
- d. Teacher

YOUR LOOK
- a. Bright and vibrant
- b. Relaxed and sporty
- c. Pretty and girly
- d. Comfy and cosy

YOUR PERFECT SATURDAY
- a. Karaoke
- b. Go-karting
- c. Shopping
- d. Museum

HOMEWORK
- a. Perfectly presented
- b. Done quickly
- c. Can wait til later
- d. Takes time

YOUR FAVE SNACK
- a. French pastry
- b. Fresh fruit
- c. Smoothie
- d. Cheese

WITH YOUR FRIENDS, YOU'RE
- a. Leader of the pack
- b. Mates with everyone
- c. One of the gang
- d. BFFs

DREAM HOLIDAY
- a. Drama camp
- b. Adventure
- c. Pool time
- d. Sightseeing

©MGA
©2024 Crayola

YOUR SOUL COLOUR

MOSTLY As

YOUR SOUL COLOUR IS YELLOW

Like Crayellow Cutie, you have plenty of confidence and don't mind standing out from the crowd. Your friends and family know you have a secret soft side.

MOSTLY Bs

YOUR SOUL COLOUR IS ORANGE

You have bags of energy and like Sunset Orange Surfer, you can't help but be outgoing. You love to try new things and make friends super-easily.

MOSTLY Cs

YOUR SOUL COLOUR IS STRAWBERRY

You love to spend time on your appearance and like Wild Strawberry Star you enjoy being pampered. You're known for your witty and clever outlook.

MOSTLY Bs

YOUR SOUL COLOUR IS PERIWINKLE

You're very organised and like to be on top of things. Just like Precious Periwinkle, you like to look before you leap, but always make times for those you love.

©MGA
©2024 Crayola

THE BEST YEAR EVA!

Make sure your year is as full of fun as the Crayola crew!

TICK OFF EACH OF THESE THINGS AS SOON AS YOU MANAGE IT.

This year I will...

1. Raise some money for charity
2. Laugh so hard, my sides hurt
3. Master a new recipe
4. Make at least one new friend
5. Visit a place I've never been to before
6. Make someone a birthday present
7. Overcome one of my fears
8. Try a new style

©MGA ©2024 Crayola

MIRROR MIRROR

Draw a picture of yourself in Wild Strawberry Star's mirror. Then write three affirmations that you want to come true this year.

We've done one for you!

↳ I AM ENOUGH!
....

1. ....
2. ....
3. ....

5 things to stop worrying about this year.

Write down your five biggest worries in the balloons, then let them float away.

1.
2.
3.
4.
5.

©MGA
©2024 Crayola

45

COLOUR CREATIONS

1 HALF 'N' HALF!

Draw the other half of Wild Strawberry Star.

2 PART OF THE FAM!

Draw yourself as a L.O.L. B.B.

©MGA
©2024 Crayola

Grab your fave Crayola colours and get creative with these fun activities.

3 SIP IN STYLE!

Doodle a fabulous design on Crayellow Cutie's cup.

4 HAPPENING HEADWEAR

Design another cool beanie for Electric Lime Skater.

MEET SUNSET ORANGE SURFER

SURF IS ALWAYS UP FOR THIS B.B.

GRAB YOUR CRAYOLA TOOLS AND ADD A FIERCE PATTERN TO THIS SURFBOARD.

WHICH OF SUNSET ORANGE SURFER'S ACCESSORIES, SUN CREAM OR SUNGLASSES, ARE PICTURED THE MOST?

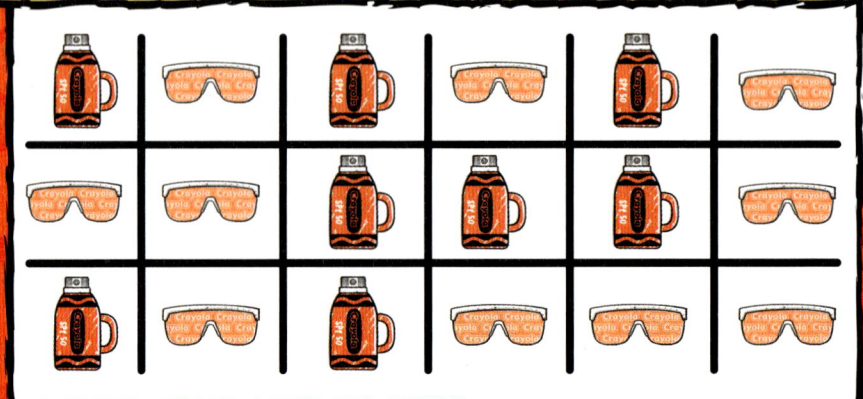

WRITE YOUR ANSWER HERE. ....

Answers on pages 76–77.

©MGA
©2024 Crayola

STRIPES ARE ALWAYS IN WHEN IT COMES TO SPORTSWEAR.

SUNSET ORANGE SURFER KNOWS THAT SUN CREAM IS ALWAYS A GOOD LOOK.

©MGA
©2024 Crayola

49

COLOUR QUEEN!

Grab a friend and your Crayola tools, and get playing!

YOU WILL NEED

- A friend to play with
- Crayons
- Dice or dice app
- Counters

INSTRUCTIONS

1. Choose Side A or Side B.
2. Place your counters on START.
3. Take turns to roll the dice and move the number shown.
4. If you land on a picture on your side of the board, colour it in.
5. The first player to colour all of their pictures wins!

©MGA ©2024 Crayola

START

SIDE B

- 1 — ROLL AGAIN
- 2
- 3
- 4 — MISS A TURN
- 5
- 6
- 7

Super shadows

Which of the shadows below matches this picture of Queen Bee and her pup exactly?

a

b

c

d

e

Answers on pages 76–77.

SAY CHEESE!

Unzip your pencil case and colour these fabulous B.B. photos!

ART IS LIFE

COLOUR MY FEELINGS!

Make a colour mood wheel to show your emotions.

We all feel different emotions every single day. Sometimes our emotions can feel like a rollercoaster.

INSTRUCTIONS

1. Think about a time when you've felt angry. Close your eyes and remember how it feels. What did it feel like in your body? What colour comes to mind when you think of that feeling? Pick up the crayon that represents how you feel and scribble with it or make a quick design here.

2. Next, think about a time when you've felt happy. Close your eyes and remember how it felt. Now think about a colour that represents how you feel and scribble or make a quick design here.

3. Now it's time to fill in your colour wheel on the opposite page.

4. Read each emotion aloud. Close your eyes and remember a time when you felt like that. Pick a colour that represents that feeling for you. You can also doodle designs that show that feeling.

5. Move around the board, doing the same for each emotion, until the entire wheel is filled out.

6. Then carefully cut out your colour wheel and put it somewhere safe.

7. If you ever feel overwhelmed by emotion, you can use this awesome wheel to show how you are feeling. If you don't want to talk, that's OK, just pull out your colour wheel and point to how you feel.

©MGA ©2024 Crayola

YOU WILL NEED YOUR:

CRAYOLA KIT

***SAFETY SCISSORS**

*Always ask a grown-up before using scissors.

Cut along the dotted line ↘

If you don't want to cut up your book, trace, photocopy or scan and print this page instead.

- HAPPY
- ANGRY
- WORRIED
- PROUD
- SAD
- EXCITED
- SURPRISED
- SCARED

©MGA
©2024 Crayola

FABULOUS FASHION!

Get your **FASHION ON** and fit all the words opposite into the grid.

Fabulous

1. ~~FASHION~~
2. PATTERN
3. FABULOUS
4. STYLE
5. GLAM
6. ICONIC
7. GLITTER
8. FIERCE
9. RETRO
10. SHINE
11. RUNWAY
12. SEQUIN

CROSS THE WORDS OUT AS YOU GO.

WE'VE DONE ONE FOR YOU!

FASHION

Answers on pages 76–77.

10 WAYS TO BE CREATIVE EVERY DAY!

Finding that creative spark couldn't be easier!

1. GET COLOURING

Grab a colouring sheet or pop a small colouring book together with your Crayola tools in your bag for on the go. Find 15 mins every day to put up your feet and colour away.

2. ART JOURNAL

Grab a sketchbook and fill it up with things that you love. It could be doodles, sketches, postcards that inspire you or even funny sayings. What will you put in yours?

3. EAT A NEW FOOD

Give your tastebuds a creative treat by choosing a brand new food at the supermarket. You never know, it might turn out to be your new favourite food.

4. SCAVENGER HUNT

Get outside and find sticks, pinecones or different-shaped pebbles. See what cool creations you can make out of them once you get home.

©MGA
©2024 Crayola

5 CREATIVITY JAR

Write out ten or more activities you love or would like to try on slips of paper. Fold them, and place in a jar. Whenever you have time, randomly pick a slip and do the activity.

6 HAPPY BOOK

Draw what has made you happy or grateful every single day. What magical stories will your pictures tell? Post them up on the fridge where you can see them.

7 DAYDREAM

Set aside time every day to daydream. Relax and do nothing and let your ideas flow. You'll be amazed at where your imagination takes you.

8 WRITE A STORY

Think of a word and write a short story about it. No pressure. No need to share. It's just a chance to get those creative juices flowing.

9 GET CIRCLING

Draw 30 circles onto a piece of paper. Now in one minute, make as many as you can into objects. You could draw the sun, the Earth, a cat — whatever you like. See where your imagination takes you.

10 GO OUTSIDE

Spending time outside is guaranteed to set your mind up for success. Fresh air opens up space for lots of thoughts and actions.

Loud and Proud

Get a bit of L.O.L. inspo in your life by colouring these feel-good call-outs.

ART IS LIFE

CUTE & KIND

BE YOU

LET'S BE KIND

PIECES OF PUZZLES

Work out which pieces complete this cute jigsaw and draw lines to put them back in place.

Answers on pages 76-77.

THE FINISHING TOUCHES!

Add a cute pattern to these slippers for Sleepybones.

What charms would work best on this bracelet for KittyQueen? Draw them!

Grab your Crayola tools and let your creativity run wild.

Add a finishing touch to Neon Q.T.'s tights. Polka dots, stripes or tartan? You decide!

This bag needs some colour to go with PopHeart's outfit.

How it works is up to you!

MEET SKY BLUE DREAMER

THIS B.B. IS A DREAM OF A FASHION QUEEN!

CIRCLE EVERY SECOND LETTER TO FIND OUT WHAT SKY BLUE DREAMER IS DREAMING OF.

START → A**F**PUSNOWTIQT...

WRITE YOUR ANSWER HERE

____ ____ _____

FINISH

Answers on pages 76–77

©MGA
©2024 Crayola

GRAB YOUR CRAYOLA TOOLS AND COLOUR HER IN.

HER STYLISH EYE MASK ALWAYS GUARANTEES A SLEEP FULL OF THE BEST DREAMS.

SKY BLUE DREAMER ALWAYS HAS THE MOST STYLISH NIGHT WEAR

©2024 Crayola ©MGA

COLOUR THERAPY

Colour in this cutie using your Crayola tools. Then read on to see what the colours you used say about you!

LIFE'S A CANVAS

If you used the following colours it means...

ORANGE
You like new trends, dancing, energetic sports and fresh fruit. Your personality is so bright, you gotta wear shades and you feel at home on the beach and the footy field.

PINK
You're sugary sweet and you know your way around a cute hairstyle. Your friends come to you for all the goss and your in-the-know take on the latest lipgloss.

GREEN
You think outside the box and you don't mind being quirkier and different from your friends. You're the first to try something that's a bit unusual and you always totally rock it.

PURPLE
You're thoughtful, sometimes quiet and mysterious, and very imaginative and cool. You're not a look-at-me kinda girl, but you're incredibly artistic with an amazing creative life.

YELLOW
You're a mellow dreamer who loves daisy chains, afternoon picnics and popcorn. Your glass is always half full because you're a sunny-side up, always smiling kinda girl.

BLUE
You're not a super girly-girl and like things to be peaceful and calm. You could stare at the ocean for hours and love watching the clouds go by. People love chilling with you.

RED
You're classic yet adventurous and when you enter a room, people tend to notice. You think food should be spicy, hair should be big and life should be bold, bright and fast.

ANYTHING ELSE
You're a free spirit. You never follow the crowd, preferring to go your own way. People know they can always rely on you for something super-interesting to say.

©MGA
©2024 Crayola

Shh! Top secret!

TOP SECRET

1. What is Cotton Candy Sweetie saying?

CODE KEY

1	2	3	4	5	6	7	8	9	10
K	A	B	N	F	I	D	M	G	E

Write your answer here.

_3 10   1 6 4 7_

2. What message has Sunset Orange Surfer left you?

CODE KEY

A	B	C	D	E	F	G	H	I	J	K	L	M
N	O	P	Q	R	S	T	U	V	W	X	Y	Z

Write your answer here.

Answers on pages 76–77.

The B.B.s have left some secret messages for you. Can you work them out?

USE THE CODE KEYS TO HELP YOU.

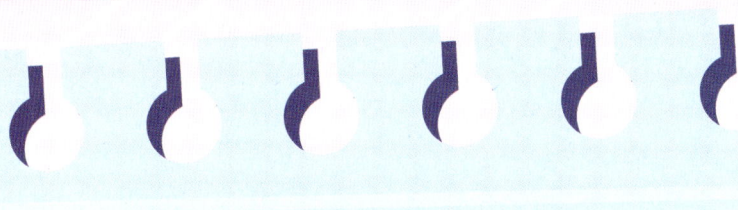

3. Say what you see to crack Sky Blue Dreamer's secret code.

You are mill1ion.

....

....

4. Make up your own code and write a message to Orchid Blossom.

AIRMAIL

Come up with a symbol for each letter of the alphabet and draw it here.

A	B	C	D	E	F	G	H	I

J	K	L	M	N	O	P	Q	R

S	T	U	V	W	X	Y	Z	!

Now write your own message here.

©MGA ©2024 Crayola

MEET WILD STRAWBERRY STAR

THIS B.B. IS BERRY BERRY CUTE!

ADD A FABULOUS FRUITY PATTERN TO THIS DRESS.

WHAT WILL YOU ADD? BANANAS? PINEAPPLES? THE CHOICE IS YOURS.

©MGA
©2024 Crayola

GRAB YOUR CRAYOLA TOOLS AND COLOUR HER IN.

HER POLKA DOT BOW ALWAYS COMPLEMENTS HER OUTFIT PERFECTLY.

STRAWBERRIES ARE ALWAYS THIS B.B.'S PATTERN OF CHOICE.

©2024 Crayola ©MGA

FABULOUS GIFT BAG

Be the envy of your friends! Trace and make this gorgeous bag.

YOU WILL NEED

- Your template
- *Safety scissors
  *Always ask a grown-up before using scissors.
- Glue or double sided tape
- Crayons

INSTRUCTIONS

1. Use your Crayola tools to colour in your template on the opposite page.
2. Cut your template out along the solid pink lines.
3. Fold the template into a tube along the dotted grey lines. Glue or tape the side-tab to hold it together.
4. Now fold in all the tabs on the base of the bag. Use glue or double sided tape to hold the last tab in place.
5. To hold the bag closed, use the little tab that goes into the slot.
6. Congratulations! Now you can fill it with candy or a gift.

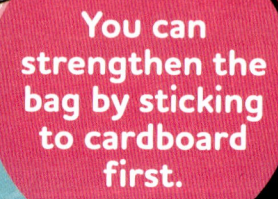

You can strengthen the bag by sticking to cardboard first.

©MGA
©2024 Crayola

If you don't want to cut up your book, trace, photocopy or scan and print this page instead.

©MGA
©2024 Crayola

ART FOREVER

Find all the arty words in the wordsearch below.

Words can go up, down, diagonally and backwards.

V	E	H	I	X	F	S	I	J	H	S	X	A	K	N
L	X	B	K	F	J	Y	U	C	Y	B	J	F	F	D
G	N	I	W	A	R	D	T	R	R	G	E	P	N	K
R	T	V	H	P	U	E	Y	Q	P	M	R	A	B	R
V	C	A	V	M	K	O	C	T	V	R	R	Z	U	D
U	R	O	E	S	Q	E	H	N	I	R	I	B	U	R
T	K	X	Z	V	C	A	I	B	B	Q	S	S	Z	U
F	M	H	I	Q	I	S	J	X	P	R	E	M	E	O
E	D	E	S	I	G	N	T	H	F	I	A	L	P	N	L
F	W	X	J	Y	Y	Y	D	A	W	M	D	D	I	D	O
U	X	P	L	E	M	Q	U	E	H	N	O	S	T	C
N	P	I	H	S	D	N	E	I	R	F	O	A	C	N
T	V	X	C	T	H	W	H	K	I	C	D	U	E	H
D	C	R	A	Y	O	N	Q	W	E	O	T	U	D	F
B	A	P	T	A	L	S	D	E	N	E	L	I	L	A

TICK THE WORDS OFF AS YOU FIND THEM.

- ✓ ART
- ✓ CREATIVE
- ✓ DRAWING
- ✓ DESIGN
- ✓ DOODLES
- ✓ SKETCH
- ✓ FRIENDSHIP
- ✓ FUN
- ✓ CRAYON
- ✓ SURPRISE
- ✓ CUTE
- ✓ COLOUR

Answers on pages 76-77.

WORDS FOR LIFE

Find your L.O.L. Surprise! affirmation to inspire you everyday!

Close your eyes, point your index finger and move it over the page five times. Then let it drop. Wherever it lands is your affirmation for that day.

- BOLD
- STRIKE A POSE
- SHINE BRIGHT *rain or shine*
- BE VIBES
- BEE KIND
- ART IS LIFE

Answers

Pages 8-9 BFF Super Search

Pages 10-11 Meet Cotton Candy Sweetie
Pictures b and e are the same.

Page 12 All The Colours

Pages 14-15 How Odd!
1. The L.O.L. that doesn't have a match is d – Jazzberry Jamm Jewel.
2. d is different to the others.
3. Hat b is the odd one out.
4. Pictures a and c are the same.

Pages 16-17 Meet Crayellow Cutie

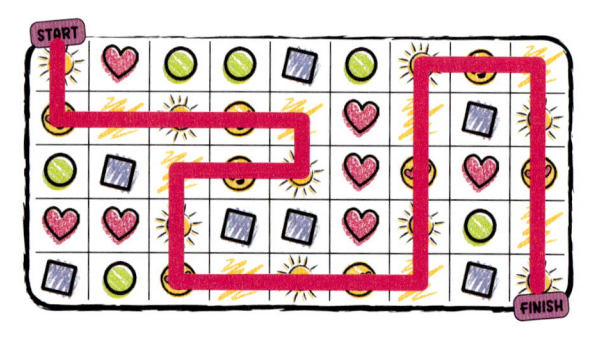

Pages 22-23 Meet Electric Lime Skater
Blue and yellow make green.

Page 24 Count in Colour!
1. + = 12
2. + = 15
3. + = 14
4. + = 17

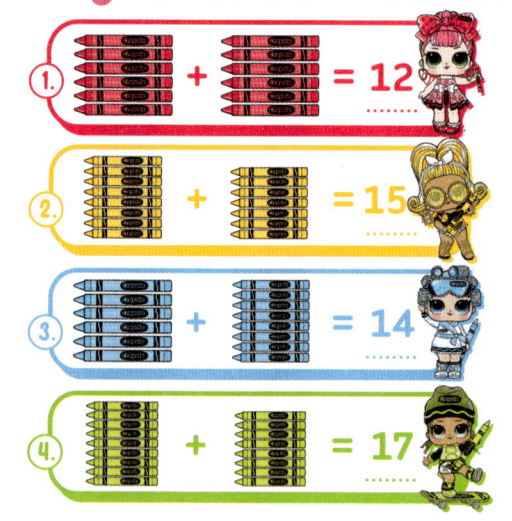

Page 25 Meet You Later!
Bonbon is rushing to meet Miss Punk.

Pages 26-27 This is My Troop!
Dropping Beats!
b and d are the same.

Pages 28-29 Meet Precious Periwinkle
Precious Periwinkle c is the odd one out.

Page 30 Perfect Patterns

Page 31 No Bars!
1 - e, 2 - c, 3 - a, 4 - d, 5 - b.

Pages 34-35 Meet Orchid Blossom
b and e are the same.

Pages 36-37 Look Closer!
Picture 1: 1 - c; 2 - b; 3 - a.
Picture 2: 1 - d, 2 - b, 3 - a, 4 - c.

Pages 40-41 Meet Jazzberry Jamm Jewel
The letters in panel b are correct.

Pages 48-49 Meet Sunset Orange Surfer
Sunset Orange Surfer's sunglasses are pictured the most.

Page 52 Super Shadows
Shadow e matches Queen Bee and her pup.

Pages 56-57 Werk It!

Page 61 Pieces of Puzzles
1 - d, 2 - a, 4 - b, 6 - c.

Pages 64-65 Meet Sky Blue Dreamer
FUN WITH FRIENDS.

Pages 68-69 Shh! Top Secret!
1. Be Kind, 2. You are a great friend, 3. You are one in a million.

Page 74 Art Forever